". . . THESE ARE THE VOYAGES OF THE STARSHIP *ENDOCRINE* . . ."

". . . **Its mission:** to cruise around the universe looking for new predicaments to get into. To search the outskirts of the galaxy for areas with less crowding, lower tax rates and better schools. To boldly go where nobody wanted to go before!"

That doesn't sound too exciting to Captain James T. Smirk and his crew when they're assigned to team up with their "next generation" counterparts. But before you can say, "I'm a doctor, not a Jacuzzi attendant," they all run into the Cellulites—warped survivors of a centuries-old dieting program gone wrong. They're big, bad, bowlegged— and more dangerous than a Snotcruiser full of Sinusoids!

STAR ~~WRECK~~
The Gene~~ration Gap~~
A PA~~RODY~~

St. Martin's Paperbacks Titles by
Leah Rewolinski

STAR WRECK
The Generation Gap

The spacy spoof
that dares to boldly go
where nobody wanted to go before

LEAH REWOLINSKI

ILLUSTRATIONS BY
HARRY TRUMBORE

A 2M COMMUNICATIONS LTD. PRODUCTION

ST. MARTIN'S PAPERBACKS

Published by arrangement with the author

STAR WRECK: THE GENERATION GAP

Copyright © 1989 by Leah Rewolinski.

Illustrations copyright © 1990 by Harry Trumbore.

All rights reserved. No part of this book may be used or reproduced in any manner whatsoever without written permission except in the case of brief quotations embodied in critical articles or reviews. For information address St. Martin's Press, 175 Fifth Avenue, New York, N.Y. 10010.

ISBN: 0-312-92802-5

Printed in the United States of America

Excellent Words Editorial Services edition/August 1989
St. Martin's Paperbacks edition/October 1990

10 9 8 7 6 5

*Dedicated to Tom, who puts up with me
at all Warped speeds.*

Acknowledgments

For research assistance, thanks to Rachel Pearson, as well as two staffers of the Milwaukee Public Library who went to great lengths checking the spelling of Murl Duesing's name.

Thanks to those who evaluated *Star Wreck* in its previous life as a screenplay, suggesting subtle improvements ("Have you considered giving it a plot?") and evaluating the author ("You're warped!")

Thanks to my parents, who taught us to talk back to the television long before it was fashionable.

Finally, thanks to all those who created the original TV series and movies, for there can be no spoof without a spoofee.

Contents

1

TAKE

OFF,

EH

"Captain's top-secret diary, Star Date 2323.2323232323 . . ."

The captain took a deep breath and continued.

". . . 2323 ½.

"Dear Diary: It's good to be back aboard the Endocrine, though I do have some qualms about sharing the helm with another captain."

Capt. Jean-Lucy Ricardo pressed the "pause" button on his Dictaphone and surveyed the Bridge. Leadership came naturally to him. He stood out among the crew members, with his commanding presence, authoritative voice and bald head.

His crew bustled around the Bridge, preparing for launch. The color of their uniforms indicated their function in the mission: red for commanding officers, blue for support staff, orange for Personnel Department, yellow for Marketing, and black pinstripes for Accounting. Many of them wore miniskirts, including some of the women.

Capt. Ricardo resumed his dictation.

"Nevertheless, I will do my best to comply with Starfreak's order to share this mission with Capt. Smirk." Capt. Ricardo pressed the "pause" button again and muttered, "That old goat."

All of Starfreak Command had been surprised when Capt. James T. Smirk and his crew suddenly came out of retirement. Starfreak Command was even more surprised when Capt. Smirk insisted on sharing this mission with the current crew of the USS Endocrine. It was an offer Starfreak couldn't refuse, since Smirk owned a majority interest in its stock.

Ricardo sighed. Time to get down to business. He began the status check with his Bridge officers.

"Counselor Troit, have you finished testing the psychological readiness of the crew?"

"They're all eager to go, captain," she replied, then lowered her voice and added, "except for the little matter of the intense hostility, insane jealousy and deeply rooted territoriality which we all feel toward Capt. Smirk's crew, as you and I discussed yesterday."

Counselor Deanna Troit was extraordinarily sensitive to others' emotions, thanks to her Betavoid heritage. The talent had earned her the post of Ship's Shrink. It also came in handy for judging aliens the Endocrine encountered during its missions. Troit could tell whether they came in peace or had some ulterior motive, like trying to sell the crew a set of encyclopedias.

"Forget the hostility for now, counselor," the captain replied, his jaw clenched. "We're all adults here, and if a bunch of space jockeys who've spent the last 80 years lollygagging around suddenly want to take over our ship . . ."—his voice had been rising; he paused and shook his head to calm himself—"I'm sure we can handle this like reasonable human beings."

Troit shrugged and turned away briskly. A moment later, her ample bosom caught up with the rest of her body and turned away also. She sat down in one of the three command chairs at the center of the Bridge.

Capt. Ricardo resumed his status check.

"Have the on-board preparations been completed, Number 1?"

Commander Wilson Piker, your basic tall, dark and handsome hunk, was standing at the rear of the Bridge. He stepped dramatically down the curved ramp to the command center and stopped in front of Capt. Ricardo. With feet planted apart, shoulders squared, head cocked to one side and hands clenched into fists, Piker announced, "Ready, sir!"

Capt. Ricardo stared at him for a long moment, contemplating the key role his First Officer played in the ship's operations. Whenever a crisis arose, Piker was always the first to step forward and strike a dramatic pose.

Ricardo was more than satisfied with Piker's on-the-job performance, but often he wished Piker wasn't quite so . . . so . . . generic. The quality had earned him the nickname of Number 1.

Ricardo turned to the forward section of the Bridge. Seated at a console on the right was Lieutenant Commander Dacron, an android who looked amazingly human except for one teeny detail: his skin was as white as a sheet.

"Status report, Mr. Dacron," the captain ordered.

"Ground crew reports loading is completed, sir," Dacron replied.

At a similar console to the left was the ship's

pilot, Ensign Westerly Flusher. Westerly was the youngest acting ensign in Starfreak and the only starship pilot with a bedtime curfew. Westerly checked and rechecked his console, trying not to look cute.

"Engineering," said Capt. Ricardo to the intercom, "everything set for takeoff?"

"Ready to go, captain," replied Lt. Georgie LaForgery from his post in the Engine Room.

Georgie had recently been promoted to chief engineer, a highly technical position which required him to wheel his chair around so he could press buttons on several consoles. It was a big step up from his previous job of ship's pilot, for which he'd had only one console and a chair that was bolted to the floor.

Capt. Ricardo thought back to the day he and Georgie met, shortly after Starfreak had assigned him his crew. When he realized that his new pilot was blind, he nearly swallowed his teeth.

But Georgie had worked out fine. His visual prosthesis, which looked like a cross between wrap-around sunglasses and a radiator, enabled him to see through solid objects and determine their chemical composition. Thus, he was the only crew member aware of the mechanical principles used in Counselor Troit's underwire bra.

At the communication post toward the rear of the Bridge, a phone rang. Lt. Wart picked up the receiver. Across his chest was a gold sash reading "Mr. Universe, A.D. 2368." The Kringle listened to the caller, grunted, and hung up.

"Captain," he announced, "the old farts . . . er, our new crewmates have boarded."

"Very well, Mr. Wart," said the captain. "Ensign Flusher, initiate launch sequence."

It was the usual backup at the
subspace on-ramp.

"Aye, sir," Westerly replied.

The precocious youngster was well prepared for this complex task. On the console in front of him was a button with a picture of a key on it. Westerly pressed it. The Endocrine's engine turned over.

"Launch sequence initiated, sir," Westerly said.

"Engage!" ordered the captain.

Westerly pressed a button showing an arrow pointing upward.

The USS Endocrine rose from the launch pad and headed into the sky.

"Set course bearing 100.7 mark 3.14. Speed: Warped 3."

"Aye, sir," Westerly replied, pressing more buttons.

In the darkness of space, the ship's thrusters glowed as the engine kicked in. The ship blasted away, leaving behind only dual streaks of light from the thrusters.

Stars dotted the vast blackness surrounding them. Planets moved by in graceful orbits. From somewhere in the depths of space came the haunting notes of a musical introduction.

"Space," intoned Capt. Ricardo. There was a long pause.

"The final frontier," Piker provided in a stage whisper.

"What?" grunted Ricardo. "What did you say, Number 1?"

"Your line, sir," Piker offered. "The line goes, 'Space, the final frontier.' "

"That's not what I was going to say," Ricardo growled.

"Oh. Sorry, sir."

"Now, where was I?" Ricardo continued: "Ah,

yes. Space. We need more of it. The universe is getting more crowded by the minute."

As he spoke, the Endocrine ran into a traffic jam. It was the usual backup at the subspace on-ramp.

The Endocrine crawled along with the merging traffic: starships, satellites, a blimp, the Wicked Witch of the West riding her broom, flying super-heroes, and a Snoopy balloon from Macy's Thanksgiving parade. An overhead sign read "Ve-hicles under Warped 5, use right lane."

As traffic began moving freely again, Capt. Ricardo continued his narrative.

"These are the voyages of the Starship Endo-crine. Its mission: to cruise around the universe looking for novel predicaments to get into. To search the outskirts of the galaxy for areas with less crowding, lower tax rates and better schools. To boldly go where nobody wanted to go be-fore!"

The Endocrine moved into the express lane ("Ships with more than 1,000 passengers only.") It took off with a roar, defying conventional wis-dom that sound cannot travel through the vac-uum of outer space.

2

MEET
YOUR
MATES

"All right!" Capt. Ricardo rubbed his hands together, trying to look enthusiastic. With the arrival of Lt. LaForgery and Dr. Cape Pragmatski, all his senior officers were on the Bridge. "We're about to meet the crew of the original Endocrine, so look sharp, everyone."

"Sir?" ventured Westerly.

"Yes, ensign?"

"I don't get it," Westerly said. "The original crew flew their missions over 80 years ago. How can they still be alive?"

"There's been a lot of speculation about that around Starfreak Headquarters ever since they came out of retirement," Capt. Ricardo admitted. "I'm hoping Capt. Smirk will let us in·on their secret of eternal youth."

"I'm interested in that myself," said Dr. Pragmatski. "I'd like to run complete medical checks on everyone in Capt. Smirk's crew."

"That won't be necessary, doctor," Capt. Ricardo said. "Capt. Smirk brought aboard his own physician, Dr. McCaw, who will conduct their physicals."

Dr. Pragmatski bristled. "His own physician? In *my* Sick Bay?"

"That brings up an issue you're all going to have to deal with," said Capt. Ricardo, addressing the entire crew. "There's some duplication in our combined staffs, so many of you will share your responsibilities with your counterparts on Capt. Smirk's team."

This announcement prompted some grumbling. Ricardo glanced at Troit, standing next to him. Her expression told him he was on shaky ground with the crew.

He squared his shoulders and continued in a shrill tone, "You've all taken an oath to Starfreak. Let's show some loyalty. Remember our common goal: to seek out underdeveloped real estate all over the galaxy—to boldly go where nobody wanted to go before."

The grumbling grew louder. Troit shook her head slightly. "They're not buying it," she muttered.

"All right, listen up!" Capt. Ricardo ordered. "Does the term 'hostile takeover' mean anything to you?" The room grew silent except for the snapping of Westerly's gum.

Capt. Ricardo's expression was stern. "Right now Capt. Smirk owns a controlling interest in Starfreak. If for some reason he's unhappy—if this mission isn't the fun fling he expects it to be, for example—he'll sell out.

"There's a rumor on the street that the Sinus-oids would be only too happy to buy into the corporation. They've got the cash to do it, too. So unless you'd like to spend the rest of your career in a Snotcruiser, let's try to keep Smirk's people happy, all right?"

Lt. Wart, standing at his communication post, announced, "Sir, Capt. Smirk and his crew are approaching the Bridge in the Crewmover."

"All right, everyone, this is it," said Capt. Ricardo, nervously tugging at his tunic. Wart, Westerly and Dacron left their posts to join him and the others at the center of the Bridge.

The door of the Crewmover, the Endocrine's subway system, opened onto the Bridge. Capt. Smirk strode out, his crew trailing behind.

The two captains shook hands. "Welcome to the Bridge, Capt. Smirk," said Capt. Ricardo.

"Capt. Jean-Lucy Ricardo. It's a pleasure to meet you," Capt. Smirk replied. "I've heard so much about you. It's wonderful to know the Endocrine is in such capable hands." *Hmmm*, thought Smirk. *He may be 60 years younger than me, but at least I still have my hair.*

"Thank you," Capt. Ricardo acknowledged. He was surprised by Capt. Smirk's friendliness. Was this some kind of ploy?

"Allow me to introduce my crew," said Capt. Smirk, "the galaxy's original well-balanced, multiethnic, equal opportunity team." Capt. Smirk hoped they'd remember his instructions to lighten up a little. This trip could be as much fun as the old days if they'd just learn to hang loose.

"First," said Capt. Smirk, "representing the Vultures, my science officer, main man and all-around brilliant guy, Mr. Smock." Mr. Smock nodded to Capt. Ricardo without a word.

Oh well, Smock never was Mr. Charm, thought Capt. Smirk, *but the rest of the crew ought to be more outgoing*. As Capt. Smirk introduced the others, they each stepped forward in turn.

"Representing the British Isles, my chief engineer, Mr. Snot." Mr. Snot's kilt swayed as he managed a stiff bow.

"Representing the Far East: Mr. Zulu." Zulu's Oriental features, normally friendly and open, were a lot less scrutable at the moment, Smirk noticed.

"Representing Moscow, Stalingrad, Siberia, and lots of other drab, Godforsaken, frigid regions that no other major world power wanted: Mr. Checkout." Smirk's grin grew a little more strained as the joke fell flat.

"Representing wry, grizzled people of all nations, our medical officer, Dr. McCaw—or as he is affectionately known, 'Moans.'" Dr. McCaw scowled in their general direction.

"And finally, our two-for-one crew member, representing both Blacks and women, Lt. Yoohoo." Yoohoo gave them a polite but cool nod.

Well, that was a bust, Capt. Smirk reflected. *My people aren't exactly falling all over themselves with friendliness.*

Capt. Ricardo's crew formed a receiving line.

"I'd like to introduce you to my staff," Capt. Ricardo said. "Let's meet them now, up close and personal. First, my right-hand man, my First Officer, Commander . . . um . . . er . . . sorry, but I'm so used to calling you Number 1 that I've forgotten . . ."

"Piker," his First Officer provided.

"Ah, yes. Wilhelm Piker," Ricardo said, flustered.

"Wilson Piker. I'm honored to meet you, Capt. Smirk." Piker extended his hand. Capt. Ricardo relaxed a bit. *Perhaps Number 1 will break the ice*, he thought.

Piker continued, "It's amazing to think we're

standing here with the original crew of the Endocrine. You don't look a day over 90. How do
you do it?"

Capt. Smirk seemed flattered. "Well, we don't
like to let too many people in on it—but since
you're now our fellow crew members, I'll tell you.
We discovered our secret after Mr. Smock rose
from the dead."

Piker was startled. "I beg your pardon?"

"Yes," Smirk continued matter-of-factly, "he
died. But you know the saying: 'You can't keep a
good Vulture down.' Mr. Smock regained his
health and brought us the secret of eternal life."

Everyone turned toward Smock. He pulled a
small carton from the sleeve of his tunic. "Yogurt," he stated.

"Our whole crew has been eating it ever since,"
Smirk continued. "It has helped us maintain our
vigor. That's one reason we've been looking forward to this mission. Frankly, retirement was
getting boring.

"Oh, it was fine for a few years. But I've played
6 million rounds of golf; Mr. Zulu spent over
70,000 hours fishing; and Smock even had time
to catch up on his back issues of Reader's Digest.
We're all itching to get back to work."

"Very good," commented Capt. Ricardo. "Tell
me, Mr. Smock, what is it like to come back from
the dead?"

Before Smock could answer, Dacron interrupted.

"The literature on the phenomenon of near-
death experience indicates that the subject
passes through a long, dark tunnel," Dacron in-
formed them. "He or she frequently meets with
a Being of Light, who reviews significant epi-
sodes of their life. The physical sensation of being

out of one's body also frequently accompanies the episode."

There was an awkward pause, finally broken by Smock's tactful reply. "Thank you. I couldn't have said it better myself."

Capt. Ricardo grimaced. "Well, then. This is Lt. Cmdr. Dacron, our token android."

Capt. Smirk shook Dacron's hand. As his crew members did the same, Capt. Smirk pulled Capt. Ricardo aside. "I'm afraid I'm not up on the latest android technology," Smirk whispered. "Do they all have white skin?"

"No," replied Capt. Ricardo. "We got him at a discount price. Off-brand merchandise, you know. But despite his skin color, he's fully functional."

Dacron smiled and wiggled his eyebrows as he shook hands with Lt. Yoohoo. The two captains moved down the receiving line.

"This is our chief engineer, Lt. Georgie La-Forgery," said Capt. Ricardo.

"Is that a visual prosthesis, lieutenant?" asked Capt. Smirk.

"Yes, sir," Georgie asserted, a bit defensively. "It works so well that my blindness does not handicap me in any way. *Particularly* when I fill in as pilot whenever necessary."

"You betcha," said Capt. Smirk, forcing a grin.

They moved farther down the receiving line.

"This is Westerly Flusher," said Capt. Ricardo, "the youngest acting ensign on a Starfreak vessel."

"Well, young lad!" Smirk exclaimed heartily. "And what are your duties aboard the Endocrine?"

"I hang around the Bridge, sir, piloting the ship and just generally trying to be helpful," Westerly said in his earnest Eddy Haskell tone.

"It works so well that my blindness
does not handicap me
in any way."

Next in line was Wart. *This is going to be touchy,* thought Capt. Ricardo.

"As you know, Capt. Smirk, Kringles have been admitted to the federation," Capt. Ricardo began. "We've come a long way since the days of warfare between . . ."

"Say no more," Capt. Smirk interrupted, extending his hand. "You must be Lt. Warp."

"Wart," the Kringle growled, tightening the handshake into a viselike grip.

"Pleased . . . to . . . meet . . . you," Capt. Smirk wheezed, his face turning red. Wart released his hand, and Smirk winced.

"This is Dr. Cape Pragmatski," Capt. Ricardo continued as they moved on. "She's been our chief medical officer ever since Westerly's mother, Beverage Flusher, was kicked upstairs by the high command."

"Nice to meet you, Dr. Pragmatski." She wasn't wasting any facial muscles on excessive smiling, Smirk observed. "You and Dr. McCaw should get on famously. Might even start a group practice, eh?"

Dr. Pragmatski's face grew even stonier. "I hardly think so, Capt. Smirk," she replied.

They moved on to the last person in line.

"Capt. Smirk, this is Counselor Deanna Troit."

Capt. Smirk took her hand. "So very pleased to meet you, Counselor Troit."

Troit smiled. "My friends call me Dee."

"Dee Troit. Lovely." Smirk kissed her hand and continued to clasp it as they talked.

"What does the title of Counselor signify?" He gave her his sure-fire dreamy look—the one he liked to think of as "setting my gaze on 'stun.' "

"I counsel the captain in matters of politics, human relations, and anything to do with emotions.

As a Betavoid, I can sense the emotions of others."

Smirk's smile had taken on a definitely sappy quality. "Ah. So you can tell, then, what I'm feeling for you right at this moment?"

Troit blushed. "Yes, but perhaps I shouldn't identify your emotion out loud. It's rather personal. I don't wish to embarrass you."

"How very quaint—a gentlewoman who speaks delicately in matters of the heart. I feel as if you already know me very well, Counselor Troit, that you can tell what motivates me, what . . ." he paused meaningfully, ". . . moves me."

"Indeed, captain," Troit responded.

Capt. Smirk kissed her hand again and gazed deeply into her eyes. Then he moved away.

Troit leaned over toward Dr. Pragmatski and whispered, "Raging hormones."

Capt. Smirk surveyed the surroundings. "Quite an impressive Bridge, Capt. Ricardo. You have so many more buttons and dials and fancy displays than we had. It's so much cozier in here, too. And new carpeting—nice touch. I like this."

"Thank you," said Capt. Ricardo. "Let's take our stations, shall we?"

There was a subtle but fierce scramble for chairs at the science stations in the back, leaving Zulu and Checkout standing. Things were just as awkward, though considerably more polite, in the center of the Bridge. Capt. Ricardo, Capt. Smirk, Piker, Troit and Smock had only three command chairs between them.

"Number 1, take care of this, will you?" said Capt. Ricardo. "Get us two more chairs."

"Sir, we don't have any extra equipment on board," Piker reminded him. "Fuel-economy measures from Starfreak, you'll recall."

"Then get something from the HolidayDeck."

"Yes, sir."

A short time later, the five of them sat in Piker's "solution" to the seating problem: a semi-circular restaurant booth made of tufted plastic, complete with a pedestal table in front of it. Capt. Ricardo, seated in the center of the elbow-to-elbow quintet, put on a happy face and tried to make the best of it.

"Well, here we are," he chirped. "Now, I like to run a democratic Bridge. I often consult with my staff. So! What Warped speed should we maintain for the first sector of our voyage?"

Everyone in Capt. Smirk's crew looked at Capt. Ricardo in astonishment. Capt. Smirk's jaw dropped open slightly, and Mr. Smock's frown deepened.

"Capt. Smirk, you first," Capt. Ricardo invited.

Capt. Smirk recovered his composure and replied diplomatically, "Let's go with Warped 6."

"Mr. Smock, what do you say?" asked Capt. Ricardo.

"Warped 6 should prove satisfactory," Smock answered.

"Number 1?"

"I'm kind of partial to Warped 5 myself," Piker asserted.

Capt. Ricardo polled everyone on the Bridge in turn, then asked Dacron to calculate the average of all responses. It turned out to be Warped 5.375.

"Ensign Flusher, maintain Warped 5.375," the captain ordered.

"Aye, sir."

"Captain," Counselor Troit broke in, "request permission to leave the Bridge."

"Leave the Bridge? Why, counselor? We were just getting comfortable."

Troit fidgeted in the booth and mumbled something.

"What's that, counselor? Speak up, will you?"

"I said, I have to go to the bathroom," she hissed.

"Oh. Very well."

The others shifted aside and left the booth, except for Capt. Smirk, who slid over to the center. He leaned back, spreading his arms across the seat and making himself comfortable.

"Aahhh," he exhaled. "It's good to be back in the saddle again."

Capt. Smirk rubbed his hands over the upholstery. In the seam between the back and the seat, he found something and pulled it out. It was a coin.

"Hmmm," he mused, "somebody lost a quarter here."

Capt. Smirk shifted into his command posture and intoned, "Mr. Smock! At this Warped speed, how long until we reach the Crabby Nebula?"

Mr. Smock began, "Approximately t—"

Dacron interrupted. "Precisely 23 Earth hours, sir." From his post at the front of the Bridge, Dacron did not notice Smock glaring at the back of his head.

"Thank you, Mr. Dacron," said Capt. Smirk.

"Well," said Capt. Ricardo, "now that we're underway, I think it's time my people gave the original crew a tour."

"Terrific idea!" Capt. Smirk responded. The rest of his crew looked as if someone had suggested they have their wisdom teeth pulled.

"Everyone on my crew: get together with your counterparts and show them your department," instructed Capt. Ricardo. "That includes you, Ensign Flusher; you may put the ship on automatic pilot for now. I'll tour with Capt. Smirk, of course. Mr. Dacron, you have the Bridge."

"Aye, sir." Out of the corner of his eye, Dacron watched them leave. When the Crewmover door closed behind them, he glanced around the Bridge, making sure he was alone.

Then Dacron pressed a button on his console. Its display screen became a small TV monitor. Dacron's favorite daytime show, "As the Starship Turns," was just beginning.

"Oh, Trevor, Trevor . . ." moaned an actress on the soundtrack.

"Oh, Tiffany, Tiffany . . ." responded her partner.

Dacron watched their embrace with great interest. Without taking his eyes from the screen, he reached into a concealed compartment in his chair and pulled out a can of soda.

"Trevor, I have something very important to tell you."

Dacron leaned forward, entranced.

"I . . . I'm going to have your baby."

I knew it, I knew it! Dacron exulted to himself. *Hot dog! The plot is really thickening today.*

Dacron sat back in satisfaction and took a long swig of soda.

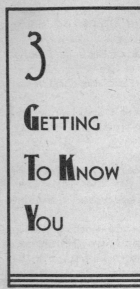

3

GETTING

TO KNOW

YOU

Capt. Ricardo and Capt. Smirk stepped into the Crewmover. "Destination, please," said the Crewmover's automated voice.

"Officers' quarters," instructed Capt. Ricardo.

"Thank you," responded the Crewmover, which then began playing its taped announcement. "Welcome to the Crewmover system. For your safety and comfort, please follow these few simple guidelines. Keep your arms and legs inside the compartment at all times . . ."

Capt. Ricardo scowled. "Computer, fast-forward through these instructions."

"Yes, captain," the computer responded. There were squiggly sounds as the audio tape advanced. Then the Crewmover continued:

"When you leave, please check the compartment to be sure you have taken all your belongings, including small children, heh, heh, heh."

"All the way to the end, Computer," the captain snapped.

Squiggly tape-advance sounds resumed. Then

the Crewmover speakers played an easy-listening version of "Tie a Yellow Ribbon 'Round the Old Oak Tree."

"So," said Capt. Ricardo, resuming their conversation, "you haven't seen your quarters yet?"

"No," responded Capt. Smirk. "I was in the observation deck during launch."

The Crewmover door opened, and they entered the corridor.

"I understand the quarters on your ship were somewhat Spartan," Capt. Ricardo said. "I hope you'll be pleasantly surprised by the creature comforts we now enjoy." They entered Capt. Smirk's suite.

"Say, this is impressive," commented Capt. Smirk as he walked through the living room and continued into a side room.

"Hey!" he called, his voice bouncing off the ceramic tiles. "A Jacuzzi! Terrific!" He returned to the living room.

Capt. Ricardo continued the tour, turning on the bedroom light and stepping over to the headboard of the bed.

"And for those days when the responsibilities of command leave your muscles tense . . ." He flicked the switch on a box fastened to the headboard. The bed vibrated vigorously.

"And what's this?" Capt. Smirk stepped up to the wide-screen TV on the other side of the room.

"Dacron replicated that for me in the UltraFax," said Capt. Ricardo. "It's an ancient entertainment device called a television. When you're keyed up from a hectic day at the helm, you watch this for a while and it helps you stop thinking."

Capt. Ricardo turned on the set and continued his explanation. "I've forbidden these devices anywhere except in my quarters, and now in yours also. I don't want the crew to get into the habit of watching. I've found it's quite addictive."

The screen showed the call letters of station WYUK, and an announcer stated, "We now return to Murl Duesing Safari." As the show resumed, Murl was wrestling an aardvark.

As Capt. Ricardo reached out to turn off the set, Capt. Smirk grabbed his wrist without glancing away from the screen.

"Wait, please," he said. "I want to see what happens."

Dacron was so deeply engrossed in "As the Starship Turns" that Westerly's return to the Bridge startled him into spilling soda onto his control console.

Westerly was munching a Twinkie. "They didn't need me to show them around the ship," he whined with his mouth full. "I shoulda known that old crew wouldn't have any kids my age."

"That snack cake is intriguing," commented Dacron. "May I observe it more closely?"

"Sure," said Westerly. He walked over, leaned down till his face was inches from Dacron's, and stuck out his cake-encrusted tongue. "Bleaaahhh."

Dacron studied Westerly with great curiosity. "Fascinating," he observed. "Every one of your molars has at least one dental filling."

Westerly was disappointed. "Dacron, it's impossible to gross you out," he complained.

"May I trade you a can of soda for one of those Twinkies?" Dacron asked. Then something on his console caught his eye.

Westerly noticed the shift in Dacron's attention. "What's wrong?" Westerly asked.

"These headings indicate we are being drawn off course," Dacron said.

"Ummm. And your TV isn't working," Westerly noticed. He went to a science station in the back, opened a drawer, and turned on a small portable television hidden inside.

"This one works just fine," he called from the back of the Bridge. "You must have shorted out your console when you spilled that soda, Dacron. The readings are probably wrong."

"That is quite likely, Westerly. We could not be traveling so far from our intended direction without drastic course alterations."

"So we have something in common," Dr. McCaw admitted to Dr. Pragmatski. Her medical diploma on the wall of Sick Bay indicated that she, too, had graduated from the Institute of Sarcastic Medicine.

"Oh, you're well remembered around the institute," allowed Dr. Pragmatski. "Medical students are now required to memorize the McCaw Amendments to the Hippocratic Oath. All 50 of them." She groaned, then recited the first few amendments: "I'm a doctor, not a rhinoceros. I'm a doctor, not a cotton ball. I'm a doctor, not a billiard cue. I'm a doctor, not a Roto Rooter."

A smile cracked across Dr. McCaw's face. "My contribution to medical science," he mused, staring into the distance.

"Contribution, muy uvula!" snapped Dr. Pragmatski. "Those amendments set back cooperation between starship captains and doctors at least 50 years!"

They glared at each other.

*

"And this, gentlemen, is the HolidayDeck," Piker announced proudly.

"What does it do?" Zulu asked as he and Checkout gazed at the wide entrance doors. They'd accepted Piker's offer of a tour after Mr. Smock declined; Smock said he was overdue for his weekly eyebrow-tweezing.

"The HolidayDeck is a simulator that will create any environment we choose, complete with climate and other special effects," Piker explained.

"I'd like to try it," Checkout said.

"Certainly." Piker stepped up to the Holiday-Deck control panel. "A setting to remind you of your homeland, perhaps?"

He spoke to the panel. "Establish an environment similar to the Siberian region of Earth."

A cold wind blasted them as the HolidayDeck doors opened. Snowflakes fluttered into the hallway.

"My, that certainly is realistic!" Zulu remarked. He and Checkout huddled their shoulders against the cold as they stepped into the HolidayDeck, marveling at the wet snow clinging to their uniforms.

"Just wait till you see how authentic it looks when the doors close!" Piker concurred, beaming. He touched the control panel to shut the doors behind Zulu and Checkout, imagining their delight at how cleverly the HolidayDeck disguised the exit.

Just then Piker noticed the clock. *Good grief,* he thought, *I'm missing the start of "The Beverly Hillbillies."* He rushed to his quarters.

"Your visual prosthesis is intriguing, lieutenant," said Dr. McCaw. "How does it work?"

Georgie sat on an examination table in Sick Bay

"Establish an environment similar
to the Siberian region of Earth."

with Dr. McCaw standing next to him. "The visor converts visual input to electrical pulses," he explained. "Then an implant relays them to my brain."

"Dr. Pragmatski mentioned that this device is rather painful. Why?"

"The batteries," said Georgie. "This sucker carries seven D-cell batteries, and they weigh a ton."

"Does any external eye tissue remain?"

"Well, yes." Georgie hesitated. "Most people are pretty squeamish about it, though, so I always wear my visor in public."

"I'd like to examine the area, if you don't mind," said Dr. McCaw.

"Are you sure? It's pretty yuccky."

"Good God, man," barked Dr. McCaw, "as a doctor, I'm used to these things."

"Well . . . OK," Georgie relented. He removed his visor. Out popped fake eyeballs on springs, bouncing and dangling in front of his face.

"Aaargh! Eccch!" exclaimed Dr. McCaw. "Put it back on. Geez, that's disgusting!"

Just then the ship's engines rumbled slightly. A moment later, Capt. Ricardo's voice came over the intercom.

"Mr. LaForgery."

"Yes, sir. I heard that, too."

"Everything all right in the Engine Room?"

"I'll go check, sir."

Smock sat back in the barber's chair and tried to relax. He'd come to Hair Port, the Endocrine's salon, for more than just his regular eyebrow tweezing; he also needed time to sort out his thoughts.

When Capt. Ricardo suggested they all tour the ship with their counterparts, Mr. Smock had felt vaguely disturbed. As he reflected on it now, Smock realized he'd felt uneasy because he had no counterpart on the new crew.

To Capt. Smirk, Smock had been wonderful counselor, almighty officer and prince of precision. But Capt. Ricardo divided these functions between Troit, Piker and Dacron.

It wasn't logical, Smock thought, to have three officers where one would do. However, he decided he would have to go with the flow.

He hoped that this mission would provide some scientific challenges to occupy his mind. *At any rate*, he thought, *it surely is better than reading "Life in These United States" for the 50th time.*

"So, basically, the ship is powered by the mixtures from these tanks," Georgie explained. "The tank of matter is here, the tank of anti-matter is over there, and the tank of uncle-matter is in the corner. That, plus a few dilithium crystals to help us crank it up on a cold morning, is how we keep this starship humming."

"I see," said Mr. Snot. "And where's your Jargon Manual?"

"My what?"

"Your Jargon Manual. To use when the going gets tough."

"I'm sorry, Mr. Snot," Georgie responded. "I don't understand."

"You know, lad," said Mr. Snot, "the manual of technical reasons why the engine won't work in a crisis. For instance, when your captain asks you to blast the ship out of a nasty spot of trouble, you can refer to the manual and say, 'Can't do it, Jim. The lateral baffles won't stand the strain!' or 'The ship isn't made to withstand conditions like

"Whenever we encounter an alien
race, I find the most human-looking
female and court her."

this, captain. We must keep the retroflux valves intact, or there'll be trouble on the moors.' "

Georgie scratched his head. "Gee, Mr. Snot, why not just fix the engine instead of making all those excuses?"

"They're not excuses, boy! That's genuine engineer talk—the most intimidating language known to man. Surely you understand how important it is never to let on you're not sure how all these thingamabobs work—or don't work."

"But shouldn't you try to find what's wrong and fix it, so you can do what your captain orders?"

"Achh," Mr. Snot muttered. "You're just a brownie, that ye are."

Just then the engine made a grinding sound. In the center of the room, the pulsating pillar of light faltered for a moment.

Georgie hustled over to the engine's control console. "It sounds like we're straining against something . . . a tractor beam, maybe," he speculated.

Alarmed, Mr. Snot began talking to himself. "It'll be difficult without a manual, but perhaps I can improvise . . . yes! How about, 'No, captain, that tractor beam will wear us down to a nubbin if we try to reverse thrusters.' Or maybe, 'The hull won't hold if . . .' "

Georgie left for the Bridge to check out his suspicions.

Capt. Ricardo and Capt. Smirk stood on the observation deck gazing out into space. It was an awe-inspiring sight. Like countless humans throughout the ages, they responded with sincere emotion and profound thoughts.

Capt. Ricardo mused to himself, *They can send*

a man to the moon, but they can't find a cure for baldness.

Capt. Smirk, meanwhile, exhaled deeply and stated, "Those countless stars. Why, there must be ... billions of them. BILLyuns and BILLyuns. And I've got a woman on every one of them."

"Come again?" Capt. Ricardo was startled out of his reverie.

"Oh, yes," Capt. Smirk said with obvious pride. "A woman in every port, you might say. And I can't wait to visit more ports and meet some classy dames.

"It's been my hobby for quite some time," he continued. "Whenever we encounter an alien race, I find the most human-looking female and court her.

"No matter how bizarre the aliens, I can locate among them a lovely lady in a formal chiffon gown and a hair style fresh from the 1963 edition of 'Beautician's Guide to Hairspray.' Then it's just a matter of time till romance blossoms."

"Really." Capt. Ricardo was underwhelmed.

Westerly gloated over having a science station all to himself. Crew members were starting to return to the Bridge after their tour of the ship, but now he had squatter's rights to the chair that Zulu, Checkout and other crew members had fought over earlier. The chair was at the station which had the best TV reception.

"Where are those two, anyway?" he asked Piker as the commander passed by.

"Who, Westerly?" asked Piker.

"Zulu and Checkout. I want to get something from my quarters, but not if they're going to come back here in the meantime and steal this chair."

A genuine green and yellow John
Deere tractor was pulling them
toward a distant planet.

"Zulu and Checkout? Oh, I set them up in the HolidayDeck. Created an authentic Siberian tundra for them," Piker boasted.

Dacron was leaning back in his chair as a janitor sponged out the inside of his console. Hearing Piker's remark, he turned toward them, puzzled. "That was quite a while ago, was it not, sir?" he asked.

"Well, yes, it was, Dacron," said Piker.

"Have they been in there all this time?"

Piker thought about it.

Dacron persisted, "Did you instruct them how to open the doors by using the 'Exit' command?"

"Ummmm . . ." said Piker. He went over to Wart and whispered something to him. The Kringle nodded and left the Bridge, his expression uncharacteristically close to a smile.

As Wart approached the Crewmover, its door opened. Georgie bolted out, rushed to the pilot's chair and checked the console readings. "We are being pulled off course! Westerly, get over here to your post, turn off the automatic pilot, and fly this ship!"

"Aye, sir." Westerly scrambled to his seat.

The engine rumbled again, much louder this time, and the ship lurched a little. Georgie hurried to the Crewmover, declaring, "I'm going back to the Engine Room and get to the bottom of this!"

Dacron pointed to the windshield at the front of the Bridge. "Look! We are being held in a tractor beam!"

Sure enough, a ray of light shining from a genuine green and yellow John Deere tractor was pulling them toward a distant planet.

"Wait!" proclaimed Piker. "As senior officer on the Bridge, I'll handle this." He stepped to the cen-

ter of the Bridge, struck a pose, and announced,
"It's a tractor beam!"

Capt. Ricardo's voice came over the intercom.
"Number 1, report."

Piker described their predicament.

"I'm on my way," said the captain.

"What do we know about this planet that's
pulling us, Mr. Dacron?" demanded Capt. Ricardo
as he and Capt. Smirk strode onto the Bridge.

Dacron consulted the data banks and reported,
"The planet is an abandoned Starfreak colony
known as Cellulite-1. No communication trans-
missions or shuttle traffic have been reported
here for over 20 years."

Wart entered the Bridge from the Crewmover,
herding Zulu and Checkout, who were stiff as
Popsicles.

"Lt. Wart, open 'hey, you' frequencies," the
captain ordered.

Wart stood at the communication post. " 'Hey,
you' frequencies open, sir."

"Cellulite-1, this is Capt. Jean-Lucy Ricardo of
the federation starship Endocrine. Why have you
towed us here?"

There was no response.

"I repeat, this is the Endocrine. Cellulite-1, come
in." Capt. Ricardo waited a moment, then ordered, "Lt. Wart, send that message in all languages, on all frequencies, and to all ZIP codes."

There was no answer from the planet.

"Well, if we can't get them to cooperate, we'll
try to break free," said Capt. Ricardo. "Engine
Room! Can you break us away from this tractor
beam?"

"We don't know how, capt-" Georgie's voice on
the intercom was cut off by sounds of a scuffle.

"Collect the papers in that
baseball cap of yours—
the one you got at
Kringle Night at the ballpark."

Mr. Snot came over the speaker. "Can't do it, Jean-Lucy. The wee bit of engine we have won't hold up under the stress!"

"Wee bit of a—what the devil?" Capt. Ricardo shook his head. "Never mind. We'll have to find some other approach. A voice vote on what to do is inappropriate in this crisis . . ."

"Agreed!" exclaimed Capt. Smirk.

". . . So we'll vote by secret ballot," concluded Capt. Ricardo. "Number 1, pass out slips of paper. I want everyone to write down their suggestions of what to do. Wart, collect the papers in that souvenir baseball cap of yours—the one you got at Kringle Night at the ballpark. That's the largest hat we've got. It's going to take some pretty large ideas to get us out of this predicament."

Capt. Smirk sank back into the command booth, rubbing his hand over his eyes.

4

SLEEPING BOOBIES

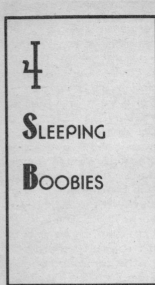

"Ready, counselor?" asked Capt. Ricardo.

"Ready, sir," responded Counselor Troit, standing at a blackboard at the wall of the Bridge.

Capt. Ricardo drew a slip of paper from Wart's baseball hat and unfolded it. "First suggestion," he said, "is 'Beam down an Away Team to investigate.' " Counselor Troit wrote the suggestion on the board.

"Second suggestion," said the captain, drawing another slip. " 'Beam down Capt. Smirk and his crew, and leave them th—' ... uh, make that 'Beam down Capt. Smirk and crew.'

"Next: 'Send the android against this alien force and let him talk it to death.' Ahem. Here's another vote for an Away Team ... and another, this one 'led by a commander skilled at striking dramatic poses.'

"This one says, 'Send a probe to see if there are any ...' " Capt. Ricardo hesitated, " '... *classic games* there'? I can't read this handwriting."

They were sorted according
to weight and assigned
a shipping priority.

"Perhaps it's 'classy dames,'" offered Capt. Smirk, as if he were guessing at what it said.

When all the votes were tallied, it was clear that most of the crew members wanted to send an Away Team. The only question was who would be on it. Capt. Ricardo had Wart check the list to see whose turn it was, and for the sake of fairness, he offered to let someone from Capt. Smirk's crew go along. Capt. Smirk himself jumped at the chance.

A short time later, the Away Team stood on the UltraFax platform in Shipping and Receiving. There they were sorted according to weight and assigned a shipping priority. Westerly, the lightest, would go Express Mail. Capt. Smirk would go Special Delivery, and Cmdr. Piker was assigned First Class. Lt. Wart, the heaviest by far, went Fourth Class.

Piker, as team leader, commanded, "Set phasers on 'stun.'" The others complied.

"Energize me!" Piker ordered the shipping clerk.

The clerk UltraFaxed them toward Cellulite-1. One by one, they materialized inside a building there, in a deserted hallway.

Westerly, the Express Mail passenger, arrived first. He felt uneasy holding an armed phaser. This was his first Away Team assignment, and he wondered again if his backpack held everything he needed: boom box, computer hackers' newsletter, a dozen Day-Glo orange shoelaces, and several Twinkies.

Capt. Smirk arrived next, followed by Cmdr. Piker.

They waited several minutes for Wart, until someone remembered he'd traveled Fourth Class. "We'd better get going; he may never get here," Capt. Smirk observed.

They crept forward, Piker in the lead, followed by Capt. Smirk, then Westerly. The sounds of their footsteps were magnified in the deathly silent corridor.

"Hello?" called Piker. "Anybody home?"

They stopped to listen. Suddenly Capt. Smirk's stomach growled. Startled, Westerly jumped back. His finger jerked the phaser trigger, sending out a beam that struck Capt. Smirk in the back of the head. The captain slumped to the floor.

"Ohhh, rats," Westerly moaned. "Am I gonna get it now."

Piker confronted him. "Westerly Flusher! The Starfreak Employee Handbook specifically forbids firing upon a superior officer from behind. I'm responsible for your training, and I view this as a serious offense."

"Yes, sir," mumbled Westerly.

"No supper for you tonight, young man," Piker admonished.

Piker flicked the communicator button pinned to his tunic. "Endocrine," he transmitted, "Capt. Smirk is temporarily out of commission. Beam him up."

After Capt. Smirk vanished in the beam from Shipping, Capt. Ricardo's voice came over the transmitter. "Number 1, what's going on down there?"

"I'll explain later, sir," Piker responded. "Let's go," he ordered Westerly.

They continued down the corridor. At the far end, a glow of light spilled out from a doorway. They made their way toward it.

Just before they reached the end of the hall, Piker extended his hand to hold Westerly back. "This is it," he whispered. "Remember how we saw it done on 'Miami Vice.' "

Westerly nodded. They gripped their phasers with both hands, elbows locked. Piker stole a glance into the room, then somersaulted sideways past the open doorway. He stood up, peeked into the room again, and nodded to Westerly. They both burst into the room at once.

"Freeze! Starfreak patrol!" Piker shouted. He and Westerly stood there panting for a long moment, taut with tension. Westerly was the first to relax.

"It looks like they're freezing, all right," he observed.

Lining the walls were several hundred transparent plastic compartments. Each compartment held a human. They were standing up and appeared to be in suspended animation. On one wall, a flashing sign read "Diet in Progress. Do Not Disturb."

" 'Diet in Progress'? What does that mean?" wondered Piker.

He and Westerly strolled down the aisle between the twin banks of animation chambers.

At the far end of the room was a reception area with a desk, several chairs and a few worn copies of "People" magazine. It appeared that Westerly and Piker had come in the back way.

Westerly picked up a pamphlet from the reception desk. " 'HyberThin,' " he read. " 'Lose weight without dieting, without exercising, without breathing.' "

Piker flicked his transmitter. "Endocrine," he said, "is there anything in our data banks about a phenomenon called HyberThin?"

Dacron's voice came over the transmitter. "HyberThin was a profit-making enterprise. For a fee, this business placed dieters into hibernation until their fat cells shrank or their contract ran out, whichever came first. The business was franchised to . . ."

"Thank you, Dacron; that's all we need to know." Piker cut him off with a flick of the transmitter button.

Westerly, rummaging around in the reception desk, discovered a spreadsheet. "Commander, it looks like this fat farm went belly-up. Or maybe I should say pot-belly-up." Westerly chuckled.

Piker frowned. "What do you mean?"

"It looks like these people had lifetime contracts that were too expensive for the franchise to honor. The customers never got down to their goal weights, yet the business was required to keep them on life support, so its profits went out the window."

Piker stroked his chin. "Come again?"

Westerly sighed. "They went broke, commander."

"Oh." Piker considered this for a moment. Then he began pacing the room. "All right, so these people have been on the longest diet in the history of humankind. But what does that have to do with the force that drew our ship here? Where's the source of the tractor beam?" He headed back toward the rear entrance. "We'll need to scout further."

Westerly lagged behind. All this talk of dieting reminded him he hadn't eaten for more than 15 minutes. And he was going to miss his supper tonight as a punishment, too. He reached back into his knapsack and pulled out a Twinkie. He didn't notice that a second Twinkie fell from the knapsack onto the floor.

Around the fallen Twinkie, the air shimmered, and the diet chambers within several yards shook slightly.

Smirk awoke in sick bay.
Troit was at his side.

Westerly and Piker heard the noise and turned around. Several chambers swayed back and forth. Their doors creaked as they swung open.

A middle-aged woman stepped stiffly out of a chamber. She hesitated over the Twinkie for a moment, then swooped down onto it, tore open the wrapping and swallowed the Twinkie in two gulps.

Within moments, several other dieters also stepped out of their chambers, sniffing the air and checking the floor for crumbs.

Westerly's jaw dropped open. Piker reached over and lifted it shut with his forefinger. Then he hailed the Endocrine. "Captain, we've got a situation here."

" 'Situation'? Be more specific, Number 1!"

"There are humans here. We must have awakened them from some sort of hibernation." Piker briefed the captain on the status of the diet franchise.

One of the dieters approached Piker and Westerly. "Excuse me," she said, "but would you happen to have any Oreos on you?"

"Number 1, I suggest you beam a few of these people on board so we can learn more about them."

"Yes, sir," said Piker. He selected three of the bewildered dieters and lined them in a row. "Five to beam up," he notified the Endocrine. "No, wait," he corrected himself. Wart had just arrived. "Make that six to beam up."

At that same moment, Capt. Smirk awoke in Sick Bay as the effects of Westerly's phaser blast wore off. Troit was at his side. Capt. Smirk gave her a groggy smile.

Troit soothed his brow. "You were stunned by

a phaser beam when Ensign Flusher accidentally fired on you," she told him. "How do you feel?"

"Wonderful," Smirk responded. "It's terrific to see combat again. I find that danger always heightens the emotions, don't you? We realize how fragile life is, how we must make every moment count."

Troit melted into his arms. *From the moment we met,* she thought, *I've been a sucker for this guy. I never could resist a man wearing Old Spice.*

Smirk, too, was smitten. There was no mistaking the signs: the half-closed lids, the syrupy grin, the violins playing in the background.

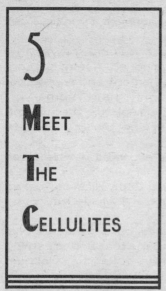

5

MEET

THE

CELLULITES

". . . So the HyberThin franchise promised that you'd 'wake up thin'?" Capt. Ricardo asked.

One of the Cellulites nodded.

"We were pulled to your planet by a tractor beam," Capt. Ricardo continued. "Can you tell us anything about it?"

"The promoters probably forgot to turn it off when they left," one of the Cellulites replied. "It was a marketing device: fly too close to the planet, and the tractor beam drew you down. Then the HyberThin people gave you the hard sell."

"Excuse me, captain," said another of the Cellulites, "but we haven't eaten in several decades. Would you have any more of those Twinkies aboard?"

Capt. Ricardo was puzzled. "Twinkies?"

"Sir," Piker explained, "Westerly dropped a Twinkie when we were investigating the HyberThin chambers."

"It woke us up," asserted a Cellulite. "There's

nothing like an honest-to-goodness Twinkie. I can smell one at 50 paces."

Capt. Ricardo folded his arms and frowned as he realized what had happened. Then he concealed his irritation for a moment and replied politely, "Of course you may have some—er, Twinkies. I'm sure we could replicate them in the UltraFax. Mr. Zulu, please see that our guests have enough to eat."

"Aye, sir," said Zulu. He escorted the Cellulites to the Crewmover.

As soon as they had left, Capt. Ricardo turned to Westerly. "You dropped a Twinkie while you were on an away mission . . ."

"Yes, sir," Westerly replied, staring at his shoes.

". . . Waking up these Cellulites, and inflaming their appetites. Ensign, this is a flagrant violation of the Prime Time Directive."

Westerly folded his hands behind his back and prayed for a quick and painless death.

The Crewmover door opened. Troit walked onto the Bridge, followed by—Westerly gulped—Capt. Smirk. *Great*, thought Westerly, *now there are two people here who want to kill me.*

Capt. Ricardo continued, "As punishment, you will go to bed without your supper tonight."

Piker stepped forward. "Sir, I already assigned him that punishment for firing his phaser at Capt. Smirk."

Capt. Smirk stepped next to Westerly and reached out. Westerly flinched, then stared in amazement as Capt. Smirk draped an arm across his shoulder.

"No harm done," Capt. Smirk remarked. He added quietly to Westerly, "You can have my supper tonight. I'm not very hungry." He patted

One of the Cellulites grabbed
Westerly and roughly
searched his pockets.

Westerly on the head and began strolling around the Bridge, humming a cheerful tune.

"Well, Capt. Smirk, you seem to have come out of your coma in a mellow mood," observed Capt. Ricardo.

"Indeed, captain! Now that I've tasted adventure once again, the universe seems so fresh and full of promise. What a rare mood I'm in." Capt. Smirk hummed a little more and began to sing, "Why it's almost like being in . . ." He interrupted himself with a grin and winked at Counselor Troit.

"But I digress," he continued. "What did you find on the surface of the planet, Commander Piker?"

An intercom transmission interrupted them. "Captain, this is the Mess Hall. The Cellulites finished off all our Twinkies *and* our chocolate. Now they're demanding we make them more chocolate, but I need to use the UltraFax to prepare tonight's supper."

"Don't we have anything else?" asked the captain. "Some nice peppermints, perhaps, or some jellybeans, or . . ."

"Chocolate, captain!" one of the Cellulites shrieked over the intercom. "There is no substitute! If it isn't here in the kitchen, we'll find it elsewhere on your ship!"

Her outburst puzzled them. "Somehow she sounds different from a few minutes ago," Mr. Smock observed. "This is not at all logical, but she sounded not only meaner but . . . bigger."

"It is possible, Mr. Smock," Dacron interjected. "Weight is regained much more rapidly after an extended fast."

Within moments the Cellulites returned to the Bridge. Dacron's speculation was correct. They

were regaining weight at an astounding rate and
had burst the seams of their clothes.

"Chocolate! We must have chocolate!" they
cried.

"Captain." Counselor Troit pulled Capt. Ricardo
aside. "I sense great desperation in them. They
will do anything for chocolate."

One of the Cellulites grabbed Westerly and
roughly searched his pockets. She came up with
a Hershey bar and tore off the wrapping.

"Hey! That's all I have to eat tonight!" Westerly
protested.

"Mr. Wart! Escort these Cellulites off the ship,"
commanded Capt. Ricardo. Wart herded them off
to Shipping and Receiving.

"We won't give them the chance to reboard
without my authorization," continued the captain. "Shields up."

Everyone on the Bridge groaned. Turning on
the shields put such a strain on the ship's electrical system that crew members were forbidden
to use blow dryers and curling irons. Capt. Ricardo always urged them to maintain a stiff upper lip in such situations, but that was easy for
him to say.

Yoohoo took Wart's place at the communication post. "Captain," she reported, "the Cellulites
are transmitting a message from the surface of
their planet."

"Open 'hey, you' frequencies," the captain responded.

An image of the Cellulites appeared on the
transmission screen at the front of the Bridge. In
just the past minute, they had grown to humon-
gous proportions. They were now coming down
from their sugar high, which made them very

Smock reached out and gave
Dacron's shoulder the Vulture pinch.

cranky. "Is this how you treat all your guests, Ricardo?" one of them sneered.

"The welfare of my crew must take precedence over my duties as host," Capt. Ricardo maintained. "We regret that our interference with your planet has inconvenienced you. However, I will not allow my ship to be held hostage. I demand that you turn off your tractor beam at once. Then, and only then, can we negotiate a solution."

"Not on your life! Before we let you go, we need more of that chocolate!" the Cellulite retorted.

Capt. Smirk stepped forward. "Surely we can resolve this situation," he offered. "I'll tell you what—you can have my share of our yogurt for the entire year."

"Yogurt?!" The Cellulites laughed him to scorn. "Ecchh! We're lifelong dieters. We're sick to death of yogurt. Chocolate!" The Cellulites began to chant. "Chocolate! Chocolate! We want chocolate!"

Capt. Ricardo gestured for Yoohoo to turn off the transmitter. He plopped wearily into the command booth and rubbed his neck muscles.

Capt. Smirk persisted. "Mr. Smock, isn't there any way we can escape the tractor beam?"

Before Smock could reply, Dacron spoke. "Yes, captain, by—"

Smock reached out and gave Dacron's shoulder the Vulture pinch. Dacron went limp. "Hmmm. It works on androids also," Smock observed to himself.

To Capt. Smirk, Smock reported, "Sir, while you were gone with the Away Team, I did further research in tractor physics. We could escape the tractor beam by spreading sand for traction, engaging reverse thrusters for 3.5 seconds, shifting forward in low gear for 3.5 seconds, and alternating back and forth to rock the ship till we build enough momentum to break loose."

Westerly beamed. "That's brilliant, Mr. Smock! Where did you learn that technique?"

"On a television documentary about winter driving," Smock answered.

"Well, there we go, then!" Capt. Smirk was pleased with this quick and easy solution.

Capt. Ricardo drummed his fingers on the pedestal table. "Excuse me," he said with exaggerated politeness. "I'm only the captain, I know, but perhaps I could offer my humble opinion."

"Yes, Capt. Ricardo?" responded Capt. Smirk, oblivious to Ricardo's sarcasm.

"We've just committed a serious violation of the Prime Time Directive," said Capt. Ricardo. "If we use force to break away and leave the Cellulites in this fix, Starfreak Command will have our hides faster than you can say 'warped speed.' "

"Oh, really?" Capt. Smirk frowned. "I think Smock's idea is terrific. And I have a feeling Starfreak Command will agree with me. I say we go for it."

Capt. Ricardo's face grew redder by the second as he echoed, " 'Go for it'?!"

Capt. Smirk leaned across the pedestal table toward Capt. Ricardo. Smirk narrowed his eyes as he issued his challenge. "Ensign Flusher! Take us out of here. That's an order."

Capt. Ricardo stood up, his jaw set. "Don't forget for a second whose ship you're on, you bloody . . ."

Piker smoothly stepped between them. "Captains," he said, "there's only one thing to do in a situation such as this, when tempers are high, the situation is critical, and bold action is required."

They glared at him.

"Hold a meeting," Piker suggested.

Soon all the Bridge officers were seated around the conference room table, except for Dacron, who was still slumped over his console recovering from Smock's Vulture pinch.

Capt. Ricardo opened the discussion. "We can't just leave now. We've breached the natural order of life for the Cellulites, in direct violation of the Prime Time Directive. We dare not ignore the directive."

Checkout spoke up. "I don't understand how leaving this planet would violate the Prime Time Directive."

"Neither do I," concurred Zulu.

Capt. Ricardo decided to humor them. "Oh? Perhaps it has changed since your last tour of duty. What was the Prime Time Directive in *your* era?"

Checkout answered matter-of-factly, " 'Don't worry; be happy.' " Zulu nodded in agreement.

Capt. Ricardo sighed and rolled his eyes. "I can see you have a little brushing up to do. Would one of my crew please update Capt. Smirk's team on the *current* Prime Time Directive?"

Capt. Ricardo's officers shifted nervously in their seats and stared at the table.

"Well?" he demanded. "Surely you all know it."

No one spoke up.

His anger mounting, Capt. Ricardo demanded, "Number 1, recite the Prime Time Directive."

"Er, the Prime Time Directive." Piker thought it over. "That is as follows: 'We will sell no wine before its time.' "

Capt. Smirk's team burst into laughter and cat-calls.

Capt. Ricardo grimaced, frustrated. "No, no! The Prime Time Directive. One of you must know it. Wart! What is our guiding philosophy? What do you say when you wake up every morning?"

" 'Go ahead. Make my day,' " Wart replied.

Capt. Ricardo's shoulders sagged. "The Prime Time Directive," he said wearily, "for those of you who seem to have forgotten or perhaps never even heard it, is: 'Put things back where you found them.' "

"Oh! *That* Prime Time Directive," Piker said brightly.

"So now that we've tampered with the Cellu-lites, we must not leave until we've restored them to the way they were," Capt. Ricardo coun-seled.

Capt. Smirk frowned in irritation. "Of course not," he said. "But what, exactly, does that mean? They were fat before they went into hi-bernation, and now they're fat again. Has any-thing really changed? They've only been awake and thin for a few minutes—*that* was the fluke! If it really matters to you that they feel thin, let's go to the Garment Nebula and buy them some tent dresses with vertical stripes."

Capt. Ricardo shook his head. "It's not the same thing," he countered. "We've got to get them rel-atively thin again—set up a diet program, get them to exercise, that sort of thing."

"We haven't really changed anything," Capt. Smirk persisted. "Let's get out of here before they blow up."

"I still feel this is wrong," Capt. Ricardo dith-ered. "We're violating the Prime Time Directive."

"Then why don't we go somewhere and get

them some diet pills or something." Clearly, Capt. Smirk was fed up with the whole issue.

"I don't know." Capt. Ricardo crossed his arms. "Perhaps we should take a vote on it."

"Take a vote on it!" Capt. Smirk exploded. "You want to take a vote on everything! Let's just get out of here and be done with it!"

Capt. Ricardo likewise lost his temper. "You know full well you have no intention of returning here, not with diet pills, tent dresses or anything else!"

"Right!" Capt. Smirk stood up abruptly, knocking over his chair. "At least I know how to make up my mind! We're leaving here, and that's that!" He stormed out of the conference room.

Piker called after him, "Sir, let's schedule another meeting to discuss this further!"

6

MUTINY

AT

MIDNIGHT

Capt. Smirk paced the Bridge. This was taking a lot longer than he'd planned.

He and his crew met on the Bridge precisely at 2350 hours, but they hadn't allowed time for removing the dust covers that Capt. Ricardo's crew placed over everything before going to bed.

Unpleasant feelings raced through Smirk's mind: guilt over taking this radical step . . . regret at having to leave just when things were going so well with Counselor Troit . . . disappointment that he hadn't been able to try out the HolidayDeck.

But better times await us, he thought. *There's a whole universe out there, ripe for the taking. Why squander our talents on this ridiculous planet?*

Finally all the dust covers were off. No one had discovered them yet. So far, so good.

"Mr. Zulu," said the captain, unconsciously lowering his voice even though no one from Capt. Ricardo's crew was around to hear them. "De-

He rushed to the window, just in
time to see the guts of his starship
disappear into space.

tach us from the saucer section and get us free
of the tractor beam."

"Aye, sir." Zulu worked the console. "Cup section detached from saucer," he reported. Zulu
then rocked the cup section loose using Mr.
Smock's winter-driving technique. "We are now
free of the tractor beam," Zulu reported.

"Set coordinates for the nearest fun-filled star
system," ordered Capt. Smirk.

"Setting coordinates at 52954 mark 61554."

"Warped speed 5," continued the captain.

"Warped speed 5," echoed Zulu.

"Engage."

The cup section lifted smoothly away from the
saucer section and blasted off.

The Endocrine's cheap security system only re-
acted after a crisis reached major proportions.
Furthermore, it had only one alarm to cover all
situations, including fire, alien invasion, and unau-
thorized cup section detachment.

The alarm system kicked in after Smirk's crew
left. It had all the standard starship alarm features. A claxon horn blared from overhead speakers. Red lights labeled "panic lights" flashed on and
off in the corridors. Steam hissed into the halls
from spigots marked "emergency steam."

Capt. Ricardo woke up in his quarters and
rushed to the window, just in time to see the guts
of his starship disappear into space. He cursed to
himself as he threw his robe over his pajamas and
headed for the Spare Bridge. Somehow he immediately understood what had happened.

The blaring horns woke Georgie. He reached
over to the nightstand and switched on the lamp,
revealing his visor soaking in a semi-circular plas-

tic pan. Next to it was a plastic bottle of Visor Scrub Overnight Soaking Solution.

Georgie sat up in bed. His right eyeball dangled from its spring, but on the left side there was only a spring with no eyeball attached. Sensing something was amiss, Georgie touched the end of the left spring, then groaned.

"Awww, not now—of all the rotten timing . . ."

Georgie began feeling around under the covers for his missing eyeball. When he didn't find it, he burrowed deeper, then deeper yet, disappearing beneath the blankets.

Wart's bedroom had a bare cement floor and cement walls. An unshaded light bulb glared from the ceiling. Directly beneath it, Wart lay on a bed of nails.

When the horns began blaring, Wart awoke at once, scowling. "Just when I'd gotten comfortable," he rumbled.

Dacron's bedroom was a padded cell. Each night he retreated there to refresh himself and recharge his energy. An electrical cord extended from his navel to a transformer in the wall outlet.

At the alarm, Dacron's eyes opened instantly and remained open without blinking. He stood up and took several brisk steps toward the door. Then he reached the end of his electrical cord. The taut cord jerked him backward, and his feet flew out from under him.

Capt. Ricardo paced the Spare Bridge. It was a dusty and depressing place. Worse yet, there was absolutely nothing for him to do. Now that Smirk had flown off with the cup section, Ricardo and his crew remained behind, trapped by the Cellu-

When the horns began blaring,
Wart awoke at once, scowling.

lites' tractor beam. For lack of anything better to do, Ricardo paged his officers, ordering them to report to the Spare Bridge.

Wart arrived first. Noticing Capt. Ricardo's robe, he asked, "Oh, is this a 'come as you are' party?" Capt. Ricardo glared at him. Wart shrugged and went to the communication post.

Dacron came next, rubbing his navel. He sat groggily at the console on the right and worked its controls for a few moments. Finally it occurred to him to wonder why they were using the Spare Bridge. "Did I miss something?" he inquired.

Georgie came in, wearing his visor, as well as a black eyepatch over his left eye. Then came Troit, Dr. Pragmatski, and Westerly, still in pajamas.

"Lt. Wart, open 'hey, you' frequencies. We'll attempt to contact the cup section," Capt. Ricardo ordered.

This raised a few eyebrows around the Spare Bridge. What did Capt. Ricardo mean, "attempt to contact the cup section"? Sensing the captain's surly mood, no one said anything, but curiosity was high. Westerly sidled over to the faded curtains covering the windshield of the Spare Bridge and peeked outside.

" 'Hey, you' frequencies open, sir," said Wart.

"This is Capt. Ricardo. Cup section, do you read me?"

There was no response. Capt. Ricardo tried again and again, but the cup section did not answer.

Piker finally arrived, carefully smoothing his hair with the palm of his hand. "Sorry I'm late," he said. "I had a devil of a time with my hair."

"No hurry, Number 1," the captain said. "We

aren't going anywhere. It seems Capt. Smirk and his crew have taken off with the cup section."

Everybody moaned.

"Mr. LaForgery," Capt. Ricardo continued, "can we break free of the tractor beam and pursue them?"

"No, sir," Georgie asserted. "What little power we have left is required to maintain the shields and keep the Cellulites from boarding."

Piker didn't miss a beat. He drew himself up to his full height and asserted, "Captain, this is a real crisis."

Since the ship obviously wasn't going anywhere, the officers left their posts and milled around the Spare Bridge.

Counselor Troit wailed, "You mean they just took off? Without so much as a 'Dear John' note?"

"Would you believe a 'Dear Jean-Lucy' note?" said Georgie as he discovered a piece of paper on the counter in the back. He read aloud the handwritten message:

"Dear Jean-Lucy: I figured you wouldn't be using the Bridge for awhile, so we borrowed the cup section. By the time I get to Planet Phoenix-9, you'll be rising. By the time I make Starbase Albuquerque, you'll be working. By the time we return, I'm sure you'll have solved the Cellulite situation. Regards, James T. Smirk."

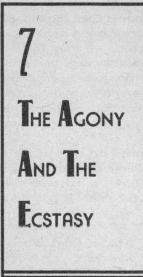

7

THE AGONY

AND THE

ECSTASY

Day 7

"Good morning. This is your captain speaking." Capt. Ricardo released the button on the intercom microphone for a moment and cleared his throat.

Things had gone sharply downhill in the seven days since Smirk and crew took off with the cup section. None of the weight-loss gimmicks Ricardo's people tried had worked for the Cellulites, who wanted only to reboard the Endocrine and devour its food supply.

The shields kept the Cellulites from boarding but required more electrical power each day. That meant the crew had to do without an ever-growing list of electrical luxuries.

The captain continued his announcement. "Today's addition to the Prohibited Appliances List is video games. Stiff upper lip, everyone."

Ricardo surveyed the Spare Bridge, which was a far cry from his regular Bridge. The Spare Bridge had secondhand consoles and beat-up slipcovered chairs. An old computer that took up an entire wall did nothing but print out a horoscope when a birth date was entered.

Absent from the Spare Bridge was Westerly Flusher. Capt. Ricardo had grounded him in his room for a month. Making him go without supper seemed too light a punishment for triggering this whole mess, especially after Smirk left them stranded here.

Today Capt. Ricardo planned to drop leaflets onto the Cellulites, containing information on every diet ever recorded. Perhaps it would help the Cellulites trim down by themselves and fulfill his crew's obligation to the Prime Time Directive.

"Hey, you party animals! This is Capt. Jim-bo Smirk with today's social schedule." His voice boomed over the intercom of the Endocrine's cup section as it sailed through the Nebbish Nebula. "Tonight we'll dock at Nefertiti-2, a fun-loving planet with some very uninhibited natives. To-night's party theme is Luau Time. It should be a blast! Smirk out."

Flitting around the galaxy and partying heavily made Capt. Smirk feel like a young man of 70 again. He'd switched off the radio in case Capt. Ricardo tried to contact him and spoil all the fun. *If they really need to get in touch with me*, he thought, *let them send a Candygram*.

Just as Smirk had hoped, on this spree he was meeting one classy dame after another, each with a more elaborate hairdo than the last. And the varieties of chiffon that had been developed since his last mission were astounding. Best of all, he still had the knack for finding gorgeous human fe-males in the most unlikely alien tribes.

Capt. Ricardo planned to drop
leaflets onto the Cellulites.

Day 10

"Good morning. This is Capt. Ricardo speaking. In order to maintain the defense shields, today's addition to the Prohibited Appliances List is the HolidayDeck. Repeat: the HolidayDeck is closed for the duration of our confinement."

Troit's mood sunk deeper at this announcement. The HolidayDeck had been her sole emotional outlet lately. She went there daily to brood over Capt. Smirk: how he had left them stranded, why he hadn't bothered to say goodbye, how she was going to wring his neck if they ever met again.

At least today she had a project to work on, one that might take her mind off him. Capt. Ricardo had asked her to contact the Cellulites on the Viewscreen and try to hypnotize them into dieting. At the very least, she hoped to persuade them to stop eating the leaflets the crew had dropped on their planet last week.

"Hey, gang!" exclaimed Capt. Smirk over his intercom. "We're headed for Parabola-X9, where the inhabitants make an art form out of the beer bash! Tonight we'll have a toga party, so don't bother getting out of bed early. Just wrap your bedsheet around you and come as you are!"

Listening to the announcement, Mr. Smock judged this a most practical costume idea, especially since he was already wearing a robe.

This breakaway from the saucer section suited Mr. Smock just fine. He knew logic would never solve anyone's weight problem, so Capt. Ricardo's pursuit of a solution seemed senseless. Most of all, Smock was happy to perform at peak capacity again without interference from that pesky android Dacron.

Day 12

"This is Capt. Ricardo speaking. I know this will be hard for all of you, but an additional sacrifice is necessary to preserve electricity for the shields. You will all have to stop using your waffle irons."

Piker was unperturbed. His usual breakfast was a quart of Power Milkshake Drink that was said to build the biceps like magic, so going without waffles was no big deal.

What did bug him, though, was the thought of Smirk & Co. stranding them here next to Cellulite-1. The situation allowed no opportunities for dramatic poses. Piker resorted to spending a lot of time in front of the mirror, combing his hair in different ways.

Worst of all, his exercise video for the Cellulites had failed. The video showed Piker pumping iron, a routine that enabled him to fill out his tight flight suit so dramatically.

The Cellulites seemed interested in weight training but never got past the talking stage. The crew monitored their conversations. After a week of listening to the Cellulites' constant chatter about how they were going to start exercising "tomorrow," the crew turned off the communicator.

"Allll riiiight! It's Mardi Gras time! Our next stop includes a rendezvous with some really with-it aliens, so pull on those costumes and get ready to roll!"

Yoohoo smiled at Capt. Smirk's announcement.

"It's Mardi Gras time!"

Not only did she enjoy the partying, but simply hanging around the ship was fun now that she was the token female again.

Day 16

"Attention all crew members. Add the following to the list of Prohibited Appliances: fish tank aerators. I repeat: fish tank aerators."

"Oh, no!" Dr. Pragmatski groaned. That meant her biology experiment was kaput. She'd spent weeks training several goldfish to swim to the top of the bowl when she rang a little bell. All that effort would be wasted now; soon their only trick would be the belly roll. Reluctantly she pulled the plug on the aerator.

That was her second disappointment this week. She'd had no luck when she beamed down and tried to convince the Cellulites to let her wire their jaws shut. She barely got out of there with her dental kit. *Well, if they don't want help, let them wallow*, she thought. *I'm a doctor, not a miracle worker.*

"Cowabunga! We'll hit the deck on AlphaBeta-Niner at 1800 hours. Tonight's party theme is 'come as your favorite fictional character.' Bring your own yogurt, and we'll mix it together for a wild and crazy Suicide Punch."

Zulu searched his closet for yet another costume. *Preparing for these parties is becoming monotonous*, he reflected.

At first he'd been thrilled over their breakaway and eager to sample the hot spots of deep space. Lately, though, he'd grown tired of their daily routine: traveling to a new planet every night, partying until dawn, sleeping it off the next day, and on and on. Zulu longed for the discipline of normal shipboard life.

Not that he'd let on to Capt. Smirk. The captain was in his glory; each woman he discovered outshone the last. *Maybe there's just something wrong with me*, Zulu speculated, *but this seems more like work than fun*.

Day 20

"Capt. Ricardo here. Attention, everyone. Today's addition to the Prohibited Appliances List is television sets. Yes, I found out that you have them, and I'm asking you to turn in your sets. Don't make it necessary for me to search your quarters."

No TV! Westerly couldn't believe the injustice of it all. It was bad enough being confined to his room for a month, but now his only entertainment was cut off.

He hated being isolated from the rest of the crew. Even the cook who brought in his meals was forbidden to talk to him.

Meanwhile, the crew continued the weight-loss campaign. Capt. Ricardo beamed down several toning tables to Cellulite-1. But even passive exercise was too much for the Cellulites, so they used the devices as buffet tables.

"Hi ho, happy campers! There's a wedding afoot on Planet Roundyboo, where we're headed. We're invited to a bridal shower for Princess Midge. Theme is 'kitchen goods.' "

Dr. McCaw scoffed. *Bridal shower, my rear end*, he thought. *This party foolishness rubs me the wrong way. And so far these aliens have all been nincompoops*.

"Oh no!" Dr. Pragmatski groaned.
Her biology experiment was kaput.

Dr. McCaw longed to treat a medical challenge more serious than a hangover, or a rug burn acquired during a game of Twister. In fact, he was surprised to discover that he yearned to talk with a hardnosed peer like Dr. Pragmatski. *It doesn't seem likely we'll meet again soon, though,* thought Dr. McCaw. *Not unless Jim gets over this second childhood and comes to his senses.*

Day 24

"Good morning. This is the captain. Today's prohibited appliance is electric pencil sharpeners. Have a nice day."

Dacron slumped in front of the computer screen in his quarters. He knew he should take a break and recharge his energy, perhaps stick his finger in a socket, but he just didn't feel up to it.

Everything seemed so pointless since Capt. Ricardo confiscated their TV sets. Since he couldn't structure his day around his favorite TV shows, Dacron plodded aimlessly around the ship. He became listless, and his skin grew even more pale.

Capt. Ricardo tried to be helpful, inventing tasks for Dacron to do, such as reviewing every obesity research paper ever published in the medical journals. But that took Dacron only about 10 minutes, and then he was at loose ends again.

Meanwhile, Troit's anger toward Capt. Smirk had softened. She replicated a bottle of Old Spice in the UltraFax and sniffed it, deliberately bringing back memories of that scoundrel. She admitted to herself that she missed certain things about him: that funny grin, the cute curl at his forehead, and the way his pants bagged above his ankles.

*

"Hey, hey, hey! Tonight we're invited to a swinging celebrity reception. And get this: Entity Magazine's 'Ten Most Eligible Aliens' will be there! Do these people know how to party or what!"

A celebrity reception. Great, thought Checkout. *That's the most intimidating kind of party. Everybody stands around checking out each others' clothes and trying to top each others' witty lines, all the while scanning the room in case somebody more interesting walks in.*

Checkout didn't need another blow to his ego. He wasn't doing well with the women as it was. Even on Planet Horsehead, where the women outnumbered the men 10 to 1, he struck out. He'd spent that evening wondering which was worse, those barfy alien women or the fact that they were ignoring him.

Yoohoo, too, was starting to feel ill at ease. This romp through space exposed her congenital defect: a complete absence of personality.

This flaw never bothered Yoohoo before. In fact, it had helped her get hired in the first place, since she would never upstage Capt. Smirk and Mr. Smock. But now Yoohoo discovered that "hailing frequencies open, sir" didn't make much of an opening line, and beyond that her conversational skills were minimal.

Day 27

"Capt. Ricardo here. Attention, everyone. We need every bit of electricity to keep our shields from failing. The Cellulites are still trying to board, and they could easily eat us out of house—er, ship—and home. Therefore, you will have to do without your Water Pik dental appliances."

The situation is desperate, thought Capt. Ri-

She replicated a bottle of Old Spice
and sniffed it, deliberately bringing
back memories of that scoundrel . . .

cardo. *Without clean teeth and gums, crew morale will fall fast.*

In the last few days, Capt. Ricardo's outrage at Capt. Smirk had begun to crumble. He was tired of the whole situation and ready to forgive Capt. Smirk, if only he'd come back.

Today it had been Georgie's turn to think of a way to reduce the Cellulites' bulk. Georgie constructed an extra-large sauna and beamed it down to the planet. "Maybe they can sweat it off," he reasoned.

The Cellulites were intrigued by the sauna. They threw mesquite onto the heated rocks and barbecued a steer in it.

After that, Georgie fell into the same funk that inhabited the rest of the crew. Normally meticulous about his appearance, now he took to removing his visor while on duty, absentmindedly playing with his eyeball springs.

"Now hear this, you wild and crazy crew. This is the life!"

Capt. Smirk put down the intercom microphone and yawned. The lack of sleep and the constant forced hilarity were starting to get to him. For the crew's sake, he tried to pump some enthusiasm into his voice.

"Have I got a theme for you: 'party till you puke'!"

Oh, for the love of Pete, what a disgusting idea, thought Mr. Snot. He'd been exceedingly crabby lately. These easy runs from one planet to the next were well within the ship's capacity. With no mechanical breakdowns and no crises, Mr. Snot worried about losing his creative edge.

Mr. Smock felt the same way. Locating the nearest party planet each day did not provide the scientific stimulation Smock envisioned when they fled the saucer section. In fact, the Cellulite problem was an interesting challenge compared to the soft life on their current pleasure cruise.

Day 29

"Attention, crew. This is Capt. Ricardo. I know this is a lot to ask, but remember, I'm making the same sacrifices as all of you. You're going to have to turn off your night lights. Cheerio, all."

Wart nearly panicked. *Turn off the night lights! No, anything but that!*

No one suspected his fear of the dark, and Wart didn't want them to find out now. Yet he worried he would cave in; like everyone else on the ship, he felt helpless and vulnerable in this no-win situation.

I'll have to manage, Wart told himself. *I'm still the bravest one on board. I was the only one who dared to beam down to the planet yesterday to try that ear-stapling acupuncture scheme on the Cellulites. It was supposed to reduce their appetites. It might have worked, too, if I'd have been able to find their ears. Perhaps more drastic measures are necessary. Nose rings, maybe?*

"Listen up, you fun-loving guys and gal." It took a real effort for Capt. Smirk to inject some enthusiasm into his voice. "We're headed for Planet Moronski, where they've planned a puppet show . . ." His voice trailed off, and he slumped in his chair.

It isn't working, he thought. *It's no fun anymore.*

The strain of making the scene at one party after another was getting to him. And the impossible had happened: he was tired of the constant parade of alien women. He missed Counselor Troit. The women he'd met on this spree seemed shallow compared to her. They couldn't anticipate his moods the way Deanna could, either.

Capt. Smirk knew what he had to do. He picked up the intercom microphone.

"Listen," he announced, "I think the puppet show can go on without us."

Throughout the cup section, his crew members looked up with sudden hope. Perhaps they could stop all this exhausting partying and get back to work.

"Let's head back to the saucer," Smirk ordered.

His crew cheered.

8 THE PRODIGALS RETURN

At first, Capt. Ricardo's crew didn't even realize Capt. Smirk's crew had come back. Zulu skillfully piloted the cup into a linkup with the saucer without the slightest bump to announce their presence. The monitors in the saucer had been shut off to save electricity, and nobody was in the mood to look out the window.

As usual, the saucer section gang was in the Spare Bridge, gathered around a space heater. They were stunned when the door of the Spare Crewmover opened to admit Smirk and crew.

"Hi, everybody." Capt. Smirk greeted them with studied nonchalance. "What's new?"

A kaleidoscope of emotions was reflected in Capt. Ricardo's expression: anger at confronting the perpetrators of their recent misery, relief that the ship and crews were intact once again, and surprise that Smirk had returned at all. Finally, pride took over. "Nothing much," he replied casually. "How about you?"

"Been having some pretty wild times," said

"It's cold because we had to turn
off the furnace."

Capt. Smirk, "but we thought we'd come back here and check out the scene. Say, why is it so cold in here?"

"It's cold," Capt. Ricardo replied, his anger rising, "because we had to turn off the furnace and save electricity for the shields."

"Is that so?" Capt. Smirk stiffened, sensing the tide of resentment in the room. His crew huddled behind him like sheep.

"All our power is required to maintain the shields and protect us from the Cellulites." Capt. Ricardo was picking up steam now. An angry flush spread from his eyebrows to his forehead and parts north. "We've been doing without video games, waffle Irons—"

". . . the HolidayDeck . . ." Troit contributed, her eyes flashing in anger.

". . . fish tank aerators . . ." snapped Dr. Pragmatski.

"Electric pencil sharpeners . . . Water Piks . . . night lights . . ." Crew members interrupted one another, recounting their own personal nightmares of deprivation.

Capt. Smirk's team went on the defensive. "If you'd learn to loosen up a little, you wouldn't need the HolidayDeck for a good time," Capt. Smirk retorted to Troit.

Simultaneously, Dr. McCaw barked at Dr. Pragmatski, "Fish tank aerators! What do you need those for? You're a doctor, not a marine biologist!"

Everyone on both crews shouted at once. The din became louder and louder. Counselor Troit, overwhelmed by the ferocity of emotion dinging around the Spare Bridge, sat down and held her head in her hands.

This has gone too far, Troit decided. She tried getting their attention. "Crew."

No one heard her. They continued shouting.

"Crewww," said Troit, louder this time. Still no response.

"Crew—SHHHAAADAAAAAPPP!"

Everyone stared at Troit, amazed at the bellow she had produced.

"Thank you," Troit added in a small, clipped voice. She continued, "You're all acting like children. We're never going to get out of our predicament by arguing.

"Everyone is at fault. Our crews have never cooperated properly. Never mind who started it; it's time for all of us to apologize."

Troit drew the two captains together. "You need to set the example for your crews," she instructed.

Capt. Smirk took on a bad-little-boy expression. "Deanna is right," he admitted. "We were out of line. I still believe in Starfreak tradition, including the Prime Time Directive. I'm sorry."

Capt. Ricardo's irritation eased. "So am I, Capt. Smirk. It's partly my fault for failing to get our crews to cooperate. I've left you too far out of the decision-making process, too. Things will be different between our crews from now on." They shook hands.

"Now, everyone else, make up with each other," Troit ordered the rest of them. They complied, some more readily than others, and within a few minutes everyone had taken the first steps toward a kinder, gentler starship.

"Here are the ground rules for this brainstorming session," Capt. Ricardo told the crews. Everyone was back on the regular Bridge, more than ready to solve the Cellulite dilemma. "You may suggest any idea that comes to your mind.

"We must avoid criticism; it inhibits the free flow of imagination. No idea is 'too silly.' In fact, try deliberately to think of silly ideas, to get your imagination working. Got that?

"All right, let's get started. The problem we're addressing is: How do we get the Cellulites back to the way they were before we came, thereby maintaining the Prime Time Directive?"

Everyone thought hard for a minute. Then Smock ventured, "You are certain no idea is too far-fetched, captain?"

"That is correct," answered Capt. Ricardo. "What is your suggestion, Mr. Smock?"

"Perhaps we could resort to hypnosis to reduce their appetites," said Smock. "I know this technique is viewed with some skepticism in the medical community, but this is a desperate situation."

"We've already tried hypnosis," said Capt. Ricardo, "though I appreciate your contribution to our discussion. Anyone else? Come now, loosen up your imaginations. Get really silly."

"What about those toning tables that people used to use for passive exercise?" said Yoohoo.

"Er ... we've tried that also," said Capt. Ricardo.

"I know!" Zulu exclaimed, then giggled. "This is really crazy. How about using a sauna to get them to 'sweat off' the weight?"

Capt. Ricardo cleared his throat. "Uh, we tried that, too. Please, make your suggestions even more far-fetched."

"Jaw wiring," said Dr. McCaw.

"We tried it."

"Ear stapling; it's a form of acupuncture," volunteered Checkout.

"We tried it."

"Well," concluded Capt. Smirk, "it seems you people are several steps ahead of us."

Those on the Bridge fell into a silent funk. Then Westerly arrived in the Crewmover.

"What are you doing out of your room, young man?" Piker demanded.

"My grounding officially ended 5 minutes ago," Westerly asserted. "Will someone tell me what's been going on in the last month?"

Troit quickly filled him in. ". . . And now we're trying to figure out how to get the Cellulites back to the way they were when we found them," she concluded.

"Dacron, review the solutions we've come up with so far," said Capt. Ricardo, trying to get the discussion back on track.

When Dacron finished reciting their suggestions, Westerly was puzzled. He began tentatively, "Why don't we . . ." and then stopped.

"Why don't we what, Westerly?" asked Piker.

Westerly looked around warily. "Why don't we— . . . no, forget it. You'll think I'm smarting off. It's not worth being grounded for another month."

"Why don't we *what*?!" demanded Capt. Ricardo. "If you've got an idea, young man, spit it out!"

"Promise me I won't be grounded?"

"Yes!"

"OK." Westerly took a deep breath. "Why don't we just put them back in the diet chambers? *That's* the way we found them. And eventually, they'll lose some weight again. It worked for them before."

There was a long period of silence on the Bridge, as each one in their own way pondered, *Why didn't I think of that?*

Finally Dr. Pragmatski spoke up. "Fine in theory," she stated, "but how do we get them back in the diet chambers? They've been anything but cooperative. They're more like the old Earth joke: where does a 600-pound gorilla sit?"

"In the zoo?" Dacron guessed.

"ANYWHERE HE WANTS." Everyone else supplied the punchline in unison.

"This calls for strategic planning and bold tactical moves!" Capt. Smirk felt the thrill of battle, even if it was only the battle of the bulge. "Ricardo, it's time for you and I to put our heads together and come up with a plan."

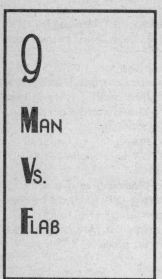

9

MAN

VS.

FLAB

Within hours, Operation Hoho was underway.

Now that they had a clear objective, Capt. Ricardo and Capt. Smirk lost no time in coming up with a dramatic strategy. And in convincing their crews to cooperate on the plan, Smirk drew on his extensive training and experience in Starfreak Method Acting.

He declaimed, "Consider the classic struggles: man vs. man, man vs. himself, man vs. the elements. What we face now is man vs. flab." No one could argue with his logic, especially since they weren't sure what he was talking about. So the plan won unanimous approval.

In the first phase of the plan, Smock and Dacron spent the night researching Cellulite behavior from earliest recorded history to the present. The next morning, they presented their information to Capt. Ricardo and Capt. Smirk.

To the captains' relief, Smock and Dacron had obviously cooperated on their research. And the

Smock and Dacron spent the night
researching Cellulite behavior
from earliest recorded history.

data confirmed that their plan would work. The operation was off to a good start.

"We believe that 20 cases of Hohos will be sufficient to enable us to achieve our objective," Smock concluded.

"Westerly and Checkout." Capt. Smirk swiveled in his command chair to face them. He and Capt. Ricardo had agreed to remove the restaurant booth and reinstall two chairs in the center of the Bridge. "Replicate 20 cases of Hostess brand Hohos in the UltraFax."

"Yes, sir," they responded, heading off the Bridge.

"Number 1, I believe it's time for your input," Capt. Ricardo said. According to the plan, Piker was to inject dramatic statements at regular intervals.

Piker hesitated. "Did you want a proclamation of victory, or—"

"No, Number 1. We're still in the thick of this, so we need some dramatic tension."

Piker put on a concerned yet determined expression and declared, "Time is running out. We need to move boldly to relocate the Cellulites before they blow up."

"Very good, Number 1."

Checkout's voice came over the intercom. "Captains, we've got the Hohos."

Another hurdle crossed; Westerly and Checkout had cooperated during their phase. Capt. Smirk nodded in satisfaction at Capt. Ricardo.

Capt. Ricardo turned toward the back of the Bridge. "Security ready?"

"Aye, sir," responded Wart and Zulu, who would provide security for the newly-renamed Aweight Team.

"Sick Bay," Capt. Ricardo said to the intercom, "ready with the sedatives?"

"It's taking longer than you estimated," Dr. McCaw barked. "I'm a doctor, not a drive-through medical clinic." Both captains tensed. Had their plan just hit a snag?

Over the intercom, they heard a muffled discussion in Sick Bay. Then Dr. McCaw continued, "All right, we're ready."

Dr. Pragmatski added, "We've got enough sedatives to relax the Cellulites for about 20 minutes. Then the effects will wear off and leave them extremely cranky, so we'd better have them in the chambers by then."

"Affirmative," said Capt. Ricardo. "Wart and Zulu will provide security backup. Meet them in Shipping and Receiving." Wart and Zulu headed for the loading dock.

"Westerly and Checkout, get your Hohos down to Shipping," said Capt. Smirk to the intercom.

A few moments later, a shipping clerk reported over the intercom that the doctors and their security escort had UltraFaxed down to Cellulite-1. "I put them precisely on the coordinates of Couch Potato Downs, where the Cellulites have set up living quarters," she reported.

Without prompting, Piker stood up and posed. "Now all we can do is wait," he stated.

It was, indeed, a tense period. Those on the Bridge visualized their crewmates carrying out the next step of the plan: Wart and Zulu luring the Cellulites outside with the smell of Hohos so the two doctors could administer the sedatives. Everyone on the ship wondered how they were doing during this dangerous maneuver.

"They can put a man on the moon, but they

can't invent a visual monitor linking an Away Team with the ship," Capt. Smirk mused.

Finally the Aweight Team reported. "We've got them outside, captain," Zulu said. "They look very . . . hungry."

"Careful, people," Capt. Ricardo cautioned.

There was another long, tense period of waiting. Then Dr. Pragmatski spoke over the intercom. "We've administered the sedatives, and they're working," she said. "For the next 20 minutes, these Cellulites will be like putty in our hands."

Capt. Smirk ordered, "Counselor Troit and Lt. Yoohoo, time for you to UltraFax down." The women headed for their task: persuading the Cellulites to cooperate with the rest of the plan. Capt. Ricardo had insisted that the Cellulites return to the diet chambers of their own free will. It was the only way, he felt, to ensure the crew was following the Prime Time Directive to the letter.

More waiting. The tension was nearly unbearable. The captains twiddled their thumbs while Piker paced back and forth, striking a dramatic pose whenever he reached a wall and had to turn around.

Finally Troit spoke on the intercom. "They've agreed to return to the chambers," she announced.

"All right!" Capt. Smirk exclaimed. "Engine Room! Mr. Snot, Georgie, are the forklifts ready?"

Mr. Snot reported over the intercom, "Aye, sir, we've got some grand forklifts ready for totin' that big load."

"Then UltraFax down and start carrying the Cellulites from Couch Potato Downs back to their chambers at the HyberThin franchise."

"Aye, sir."

Their next transmission came from the surface of Cellulite-1. "Captain," Mr. Snot said with awe in his voice, "there be whales here! These Cellulites must weigh over half a ton apiece!"

"Mr. Snot," Capt. Smirk replied, "are you saying the forklifts can't handle it?"

Mr. Snot recovered, his voice coming back loud and strong. "Georgie and I built them to take any punishment. They'll handle it, or my name isn't Sean Michael Thomas Snot the Third!"

"Attaboy, Mr. Snot." The captains sighed in relief.

"What time is it, Number 1?"

"Uh, let's see—noon is 1200 hours; add 1 hour and it's 1300; then 1400, 1500 . . . ummm . . . it's 6:25 Central Standard Time."

"Aweight Team!" said Capt. Ricardo. "You've only got 5 minutes left. Report!"

"We're having trouble getting the Cellulites off the forklifts and into the chambers," Georgie said.

"Number 1," commanded Capt. Ricardo, "take a dolly from the maintenance department and go down there to help them."

"Cabbage Patch or Barbie?" inquired Piker.

"What?"

"What kind of dolly do you want, captain?"

"Westerly." Capt. Ricardo turned away from Piker and toward Westerly at his pilot's post. "Get a dolly from the maintenance department and meet Cmdr. Piker at the UltraFax platform. You'll both beam down to help move the Cellulites."

"Yes, sir."

"Captains," Smock said from his science station, "new data from the computer indicates the Cellulites will emit a tremendous negative vibra-

"Captain," Mr. Snot said
with awe in his voice,
"there be whales here!"

tion the moment the sedative wears off. That seems to be a reaction to being placed on yet another diet of unlimited duration."

"And the consequences, Mr. Smock?"

"Computer projections indicate that Cellulite-1 will release a force field. This eruption will not harm the Cellulites in their diet chambers, but will expand outward from them with the impact of ten thousand tons of TNT, enough to destroy our ship, all crew members and any possibility of a sequel."

"Thank you, Mr. Smock. We'll sit here and worry about that for a while."

Two minutes remained.

At Capt. Smirk's orders, Westerly left his communicator turned on so the Bridge crew could monitor the situation on Cellulite-1.

What the captains heard wasn't reassuring. Tempers flared under the pressure of the deadline. There were shouts of "Outta my way!" and "Let's move it!" And several crew members seemed to be relapsing into old habits, with exclamations of "I'm a doctor, not a moving van" and "These wee forklifts can't stand the strain."

With one minute left before the predicted explosion time, Westerly reported, "Captain, we just turned off the tractor beam. We found the 'off' switch in the marketing director's office."

Then finally, with just 30 seconds to go, Piker announced, "Sir, all the Cellulites are back in their diet chambers."

"Very good! Fax back up here immediately," responded Capt. Ricardo. "No time to save the forklifts. Just get yourselves on board."

After a very long pause, the clerk in Shipping

announced, "Aweight Team has faxed aboard, sir."

"Let's get out of here!" Capt. Smirk exclaimed. He began punching buttons on the pilot's console. "Setting course 777 mark 007, Warped factor 9."

"Engage!" said Capt. Ricardo.

As the Aweight Team returned to the Bridge, Dacron began counting off the seconds to the explosion on Cellulite-1. "T minus 10 seconds and counting. Nine seconds . . . 8 . . . 7 . . . 6 . . . 5 . . . 4 . . . 3 . . . 2 . . . 1 . . . detonation."

Back on the surface of the planet, the Cellulites shook off the effects of the sedative and realized they'd agreed to another extended fast. Their irritation exploded in a burst of energy, creating a force field which rapidly expanded outward from the planet.

"Impact coming!" Capt. Ricardo cried. "Everybody grab something and hold on tight!"

Capt. Ricardo sat in a command chair and clutched the sides for stability. Most of the others grabbed a console. Capt. Smirk hustled over to Counselor Troit and pulled her body against his.

10

FINISH WITH A BANG

The explosion reached the Endocrine.

A powerful impact rocked the Bridge, and a blast overpowered all sound. The force knocked several crew members off their feet. The lights flickered off for a moment as power was interrupted, then came back on. The thunderous roar died away.

Gradually, everyone realized the crisis was past. They picked themselves up, dusted themselves off, and sighed in relief. It appeared that the worst damage was to their VCR's, which needed resetting after the power interruption.

At long last it was time to celebrate.

Yoohoo turned a knob at her station, and the Hallelujah Chorus from Handel's "Messiah" blared from the speakers.

Crew members shook hands, hugged each other and threw confetti.

Wart, Dr. Pragmatski and Dr. McCaw came perilously close to smiling. Mr. Snot danced a merry jig.

Troit and Capt. Smirk continued making amends most heartily in the center of the Bridge.

Capt. Ricardo stood smiling in the midst of it all, savoring the moment.

Dacron pointed to the windshield. "Look!"

Everyone turned to look outward. The explosion on Cellulite-1 faded to a healthy glow, much like the bulbs in a tanning bed. The planet had become a new star.

"Captain, we're picking up a message from Cellulite-1," Wart reported from the communication post. "It's being broadcast in all languages, on all frequencies, and on all network affiliates."

As he spoke, the message was superimposed on the Viewscreen. Its letters appeared one by one:

A..L..L . . .

"Alleluia?" someone guessed.

A..L..L.....T..H..E . . .

"All the way home," suggested someone else.

A..L..L.....T..H..E..S..E..........W..O..R....

"All these worms?" Dacron guessed.

Finally they gave up and waited until the entire message was revealed:

ALL THESE WORLDS ARE YOURS EXCEPT FOR CELLULITE-1. USE THEM TOGETHER. USE THEM IN PEACE. HAVE A NICE DAY.

They fell silent for a moment, deeply moved. Everyone assumed this was an awesome message, loaded with cosmic significance, since no one understood it.

Piker struggled to put their awe into words. "It appears the universe harbors an intelligence greater than yours and mine," he reflected.

"Well, yours anyway," said Mr. Smock.

The Endocrine shifted into Warped drive and blasted away.

A powerful impact rocked
the bridge.

Capt. Ricardo wrapped it up. "Captain's top-secret diary, Star Date 6256.5661. Having fulfilled the Prime Time Directive with the Cellulites, we continue our mission: to cruise around the universe looking for novel predicaments to get into. To search the outskirts of the galaxy for areas with less crowding, lower tax rates and better schools. To boldly go where nobody wanted to go before!"

Boldly go where nobody ever wanted to go before!

Leah Rewolinski's *Star Wreck* books—which parody everyone's favorite endlessly rerun TV series, not to mention everyone's favorite interminable number of movie sequels and everyone's favorite "next generation" spin-off—are turning the world—and the galaxy—on its collective pointed ear!

STAR WRECK: THE GENERATION GAP
Leah Rewolinski
_____ 92802-5 $3.99 U.S./$4.99 CAN.

STAR WRECK II: THE ATTACK OF THE JARGONITES
Leah Rewolinski
_____ 92737-1 $3.99 U.S./$4.99 CAN.

STAR WRECK III: TIME WARPED
Leah Rewolinski
_____ 92891-2 $3.99 U.S./$4.99 CAN.

Coming in 1993
STAR WRECK IV: LIVE LONG AND PROFIT